The Pony-Mad Princess

Princess Ellie's Summer Holiday

Ellie stroked the grey pony as he gently took the grass from her hand. "This one's definitely my favourite," she said. "He's the one I'd like to ride."

"Well, you can't!" said a voice from behind her.

Ellie and Kate spun round to see a girl glowering at them.

"That pony is mine," she yelled.

Look out for more sparkly adventures of
The Pony-Mad Princess!

Princess Ellie to the Rescue

Princess Ellie's Secret

A Puzzle for Princess Ellie

Princess Ellie's Starlight Adventure

Princess Ellie's Moonlight Mystery

A Surprise for Princess Ellie

Princess Ellie's Holiday Adventure

Princess Ellie and the Palace Plot

Princess Ellie's Christmas

Princess Ellie Saves the Day

Princess Ellie's Treasure Hunt

Princess Ellie's Perfect Plan

The Pony-Mad Princess

Princess Ellie's Summer Holiday

Diana Kimpton

Illustrated by Lizzie Finlay

USBORNE

For Cerys and Tegan

This edition first published in 2014 by Usborne Publishing Ltd.,
Usborne House, 83-85 Saffron Hill, London EC1N 8RT, England.
www.usborne.com

First published in 2006. Based on an original concept by Anne Finnis.
Text copyright © 2006 by Diana Kimpton and Anne Finnis.
Illustrations copyright © 2006 by Lizzie Finlay.

A CIP catalogue record for this book is available from the British Library.

ISBN 9781409566069   JFMAM JASOND/14   01433/2

Printed in Chatham, Kent, UK.

Chapter 1

"It looks wonderful," yelled Princess Ellie, as she stared out of the helicopter window. She had to shout to be heard above the roar of the engine.

"Fantastic!" agreed her best friend, Kate, at the top of her voice.

They both stared down, watching the tropical island come closer and closer.

The Pony-Mad Princess

Its hills were covered with thick, green jungle, and blue sea lapped gently on its white, sandy beaches. It looked like the perfect place for a summer holiday. There was only one problem – there was no sign of any ponies.

The helicopter landed gently on a patch of ground marked with an enormous H. The wind from its rotor blades sent up clouds of dust that blocked the view from the window.

Then the engines finally stopped and all was quiet.

"Thank goodness," said the Queen. "That journey was too long and too noisy."

"But it was worth it, my dear," said the King. "We've got nothing to do for the next two weeks except relax and swim and make new friends."

"And ride," added Ellie. "You promised there'd be riding." She was starting to feel worried. If there weren't any ponies, her holiday would be ruined.

Before either of her parents could answer, the helicopter door swung open. "Welcome to Onataki," announced a man in a brightly coloured shirt. "Hi! I'm Don – I own the island."

Ellie and Kate followed the King and

The Pony-Mad Princess

Queen out of the helicopter. The sun was so bright that it dazzled them. The air was hot and the gentle breeze carried strange scents Ellie didn't recognize.

As soon as they were all on the ground, a crowd of smiling women ran forward and hung garlands of flowers around their necks. One of them accidentally knocked the King's crown sideways, but he didn't seem to mind. He just laughed as he pushed it straight.

Princess Ellie's Summer Holiday

Kate nudged Ellie with her elbow. "Why aren't they bowing and curtseying like people usually do when they see your parents?"

"Dad says they don't bother with that here," explained Ellie. "Lots of the people who come to this island are royal. The others are all millionaires or famous film stars."

"Except me," laughed Kate. Her gran was the palace cook.

"And the maids and Higginbottom," added Ellie. She glanced back at the helicopter where the butler was busy making sure all their luggage was unloaded.

Don led the way to a white building with RECEPTION written on it in large gold letters. Inside, full-size palm trees grew in pots and goldfish swam lazily in a huge pool.

While Don chatted to the King and Queen,

9

the two girls looked around at the walls. There were photos of people waterskiing and sailing. There were notices about golf and fishing and tennis. But there was nothing at all about horse riding.

Ellie tugged anxiously at her mum's sleeve. "Ask about the ponies," she begged.

"In a minute, Aurelia," replied the Queen.

Ellie sighed. She knew from experience that that sort of minute often lasted several hours.

Don picked up some keys from the desk. "Come with me and I'll show you where you're staying." He led the royal group through the reception area and out the other side.

"Wow," cried Kate and Ellie together, as they stepped onto a wide, sun-soaked patio.

Princess Ellie's Summer Holiday

Straight in front of them was an enormous swimming pool with water as blue as the sky.

Beyond that lay a wide, sandy beach dotted with striped sun umbrellas. And on either side of the pool stood the villas for the guests, each with its own garden.

Ellie was pleased to find their villa was at the far end, closest to the beach. It was totally different to the palace where she normally lived. It was much smaller, and it

had a wide, shady veranda and a roof of
green tiles. In the garden, hummingbirds
flew from flower to flower and a fountain
splashed gently into a shell-shaped pool.

To Ellie's surprise,
Higginbottom opened
the door to greet them.
He was slightly out
of breath from rushing
to get there before
they did, and his
garland of flowers
looked ridiculous on
top of his evening suit.

He smiled at Ellie
and pointed at one
of the doors, leading
off the sitting room.

Princess Ellie's Summer Holiday

"That's your room, Your Highness. And Kate's. His Majesty thought you'd like to share."

"Brilliant!" cried Ellie. She flung open the door and stared in delight at her holiday bedroom. It wasn't pink like her bedroom at home. The tiled floor was creamy yellow and the covers on the two beds were bright orange.

Kate rushed past her and threw herself onto the bed nearest the window. "Can I have this one?" she asked. "It's great. I can see the sea all the time, even when I'm lying down."

"I'm happy with this one," said Ellie, as she bounced up and down on the other bed. Then she spotted an envelope on the dressing table. It had a drawing of a horse at the top, and it was addressed to Princess Aurelia and Kate Brown.

Ellie ripped it open and pulled out a sheet of paper. It had "Onataki Riding Stables" written across the top in bright red letters. She danced round the room in excitement as she read the letter. "Yippee," she yelled. "There really are ponies on the island and Dad's arranged for us to borrow two for the whole holiday. We've got to go to the stables at nine o'clock tomorrow morning to meet them."

Princess Ellie's Summer Holiday

"Great!" cried Kate. "I can hardly wait."

"Neither can I," sighed Ellie. She was already missing her own ponies, even though she'd only said goodbye to them that morning. Then she looked at the map on the back of the letter and grinned. "Let's go and find the stables now. Surely no one will mind if we just have a quick look."

Chapter 2

"Where are you two going in such a hurry?" asked the Queen, as Ellie and Kate rushed into the garden.

Ellie hesitated. She wasn't sure if her parents would approve of their plans. The letter hadn't said anything about going to the stables *today*. "We're...um..."

"...going exploring," finished Kate.

Princess Ellie's Summer Holiday

"To find out where everything is," added Ellie, grateful for her friend's help.

"Very sensible," said the King. He lay back in his sunlounger and sipped from a tall glass decorated with a paper umbrella. "Do you want some lemonade first?"

"Maybe later," said Ellie.

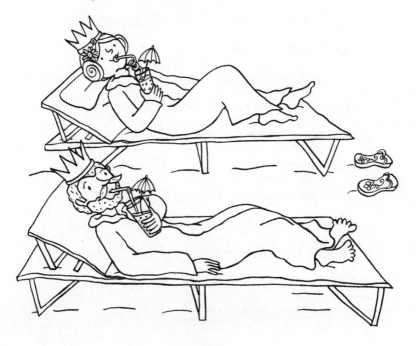

"But not too late," said the Queen, looking at her watch. "We've been invited to a welcome party by the pool and it starts at five."

"We'll be back by then, I promise," said Ellie, as she and Kate ran out of the garden. When they reached the path that ran along the edge of the beach, they stopped and looked at the map.

"Which way are the stables?" asked Kate.

Ellie pointed to the left. "We have to go along here and take the first turning that goes inland."

The sun blazed down on them as they walked. It was so hot that the sea looked cool and tempting. But they didn't stop for a paddle. They wanted to see the ponies as soon as they could.

Princess Ellie's Summer Holiday

They walked on and on. Giant butterflies
fluttered past. A lazy lizard sunned itself on
a rock. But there was no sign of any other
paths. "Have we come the right way?"
asked Kate.

"I'm not sure," replied Ellie. "Perhaps I had the map upside down." Then she walked round a clump of palm trees and found the turning they'd been looking for. The hoof prints in the sand told her it was the right place.

As they walked along the new path, Kate took a deep breath. "I can smell horses," she squealed. "We must be nearly there."

She was right. A few metres further on, the path turned sharply and arrived at a line of wooden stables. A tack room stood at one end and a muck heap at the other. In front of the stables was a concrete yard, and beyond that was a field with a wooden fence. Everywhere was still and quiet.

"Perhaps there's someone in the tack room," suggested Ellie, as she knocked on the door. There was no reply, so she peered inside. Neat racks of saddles hung on the walls and boxes of grooming kit sat on the shelves. But there was no sign of anyone.

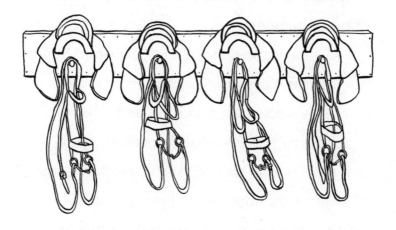

"Do you think it's all right to look around?" asked Kate.

Ellie nodded. "We're not doing any harm," she said. "We're only looking at the ponies."

They walked along the row of stables, peering over each door in turn. They were all empty. But each of them was clean and tidy with neatly swept floors. Ellie was impressed. The person in charge obviously had high standards.

"Perhaps the ponies are in the field," suggested Kate, running over to the fence.

"I don't think so," said Ellie. It looked as empty as anywhere else. Then she noticed a large shelter thatched with palm leaves on the far side of the field. She shaded her eyes against the sun and peered into it. It was dark inside, but she could just make out the dim shapes of horses and ponies. "They're in there," she cried. "That's why we couldn't see them from the helicopter."

The girls ran along beside the fence until

they were as close to the shelter as possible. From there, they could see how cool and shady it looked inside. It was the perfect place for the horses and ponies to doze during the heat of the afternoon.

Ellie climbed onto the bottom bar of the fence and leaned over as far as she could. "Come on," she called.

All the animals raised their heads to see what was happening. The two horses immediately decided it wasn't interesting and went back to sleep. But the three ponies wandered out into the sunlight and stared curiously at the two girls.

"I love that skewbald," said Kate, pointing at a pony with large brown and white patches on his coat. "He reminds me of Angel."

"But he's a lot bigger," laughed Ellie. Kate's pony, Angel, was only a foal. And she was much too young to ride.

Ellie picked some grass and held it out on the flat of her hand. A grey pony stepped past the skewbald and walked cautiously towards her. Ellie watched admiringly. He was almost pure white with a finely shaped head, dainty ears and a flowing mane. "He's beautiful," she whispered.

"Which is more than can be said for the other one," said Kate.

Ellie giggled as she nodded in agreement. The third pony was the ugliest she had ever seen. His coat was muddy brown and his head looked slightly too big for his body. Worst of all, he had no mane.

Someone had cut it off completely, leaving a line of stubble along the top of his neck.

Ellie stroked the grey pony as he gently took the grass from her hand. "This one's definitely my favourite," she said. "He's the one I'd like to ride."

"Well, you can't!" said a voice from behind her.

The Pony-Mad Princess

Ellie and Kate spun round to see a girl glowering at them. She had her hands on her hips, a crown on her head and a scowl on her face.

"That pony is mine," she yelled.

Chapter 3

Ellie stared in surprise. How could this girl have her own pony on the island when Ellie hadn't been allowed to bring hers? "Is that true?" she asked. "Is the grey really yours?"

"Not yet," replied the girl with a smug smile. "But he will be tomorrow. My parents have hired a pony for me for the whole of my holiday and I've chosen that one."

"Oh!" said Kate. "We're hiring ponies too. But we thought the person who runs the stables would decide which ones we have."

"He probably does for *ordinary* people," sneered the girl. "But I'm special. I am Princess Clara of Sanbarosa and I always get my own way."

"You're lucky," said Ellie. "I'm a princess too, but it doesn't work like that for me."

"Perhaps you don't try hard enough," said Clara in a superior voice. She stared at Kate and asked, "Are you a princess too?"

Kate shook her head. "I'm not royal at all."

"How terribly boring for you," said Clara. "I suppose you haven't any ponies of your own."

"Yes, I have," replied Kate, firmly. "I've got a gorgeous pony called Angel."

"Only one," said Clara, looking even more superior. "That's not very impressive. I've got three all to myself."

Ellie stayed quiet. She didn't want to get into competition with this new girl. But Kate did. She glared at Clara and announced, "Ellie's got five ponies."

29

Clara's face fell. She obviously wasn't used to anyone having more than her. Then she brightened up and announced, "One of my ponies is the best showjumper in the whole of Sanbarosa. He's won oodles

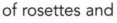

of rosettes and shelves full of silver trophies. Are any of yours champions?"

"No," Kate admitted. "Angel's only a foal. She's too young to ride."

"None of mine have ever won anything," said Ellie. She didn't explain that was hardly surprising. She'd never entered them in any competitions.

Clara smiled smugly again. Then she glanced at her watch. "Well, I can't waste any more time talking to you," she said. "I've got to get changed. I'm going to a fantastic party tonight."

"What a show-off!" said Kate, as they watched Clara run back towards the villas. "I hope we don't have to ride with her all the time."

"So do I," agreed Ellie.

They gave the grey pony one more handful of grass. Then they said a reluctant goodbye and headed back to their own villa. The sun was lower in the sky now. But it was still hot and the sea still looked deliciously cool. This time they couldn't resist paddling.

They took off their sandals and walked along the water's edge, squealing with delight as the waves rushed over their feet. Soon they started to run in and out of the water, kicking and splashing until they were both soaked from head to foot. When they finally stopped, they were both very wet and very late.

"Sorry," said Ellie, as they raced into their villa.

The Queen stared at the two dripping girls. "Never mind," she sighed. "Just get cleaned up and changed into your party clothes as quickly as you can."

By the time Ellie and Kate were ready, the bottom of the shower was covered with sand. Wet footprints led across the bathroom floor and damp towels lay abandoned in the bedroom. But both girls looked neat and tidy. Ellie's dress was pink, as usual. Kate's was pale purple and she had matching ribbons in her hair.

Princess Ellie's Summer Holiday

The party was already in full swing when they arrived with the King and Queen. The hum of conversation mingled with the gentle sound of a steel band. Fairy lights glittered in the palm trees, waitresses carried silver trays of dainty titbits and a wisp of smoke rose from the poolside barbecue.

The Pony-Mad Princess

Don greeted them warmly and led them towards a group of other guests. "I've got a surprise for you two girls," he said. "There's someone here who could make your holiday even better than you imagined."

Ellie grinned. She loved surprises and couldn't wait to find out who it was.

Princess Ellie's Summer Holiday

Perhaps it would be a famous film star. Or, better still, a famous showjumper.

Then Don beckoned someone out from the group. Ellie's excitement turned to dismay as she saw the mystery guest. This wasn't a good surprise at all!

Chapter 4

"This is Princess Clara," said Don.

"A lovely new friend to play with while you're here," added the Queen.

"Oh!" said Ellie, without enthusiasm. "We've already met." She forced herself to smile as she was introduced to Clara's mum and dad, the Duke and Duchess of Sanbarosa. They were both surprisingly pleasant for people with such an awful daughter.

"We're delighted Clara will have friends while she's here," said the Duke. "She hasn't any at home."

"I'm not surprised," Kate whispered in Ellie's ear.

But Ellie felt a twinge of sympathy. She knew how difficult it was for a princess to have friends. She hadn't had any either until Kate came to live at the palace.

Clara went red with embarrassment and glared at her father. "I don't need friends," she declared.

"Don't be silly, dear," said the Duchess, pushing Clara firmly towards Ellie. "Now why don't you three run along and start getting to know each other."

"That's a splendid idea," said the King. "I'm sure you don't want to listen to boring, adult conversations."

Ellie agreed about that. She also knew there was no point in arguing with her father at the moment. They were stuck with Clara, at least until the end of the party.

Clara had obviously decided the same. "Come on," she ordered. "It's time to eat."

Princess Ellie's Summer Holiday

She marched off towards the food.

Kate raised her eyebrows. "That girl is so bossy!" she muttered.

"I know," agreed Ellie, as she set off in pursuit. "But she's got the right idea. I'm really hungry."

When they reached the barbecue, Clara thrust plates into their hands. "You must have the fish," she announced. "They're an island speciality. They're caught fresh from the sea every day."

Ellie eyed the fish suspiciously. They smelled delicious as they sizzled over the hot charcoal.

But they still had their heads and tails. She wasn't sure she wanted to eat food that looked at her. She was also unwilling to follow Clara's orders.

"I'll have the sausages, please," she said, as she held out her plate to the chef.

"And I'll have the veggie kebabs," added Kate.

Clara frowned, but she didn't stop telling them what to do. As soon as they had filled their plates with different salads and crusty bread, she led the way to a table beside the pool. "We'll sit here," she insisted. "We can play 'spot the celebrity' while we eat."

Ellie and Kate soon discovered that Clara was much better at that game than they were. She kept pointing out film stars, singers and actors they hadn't recognized.

Princess Ellie's Summer Holiday

The more people she spotted, the more smug she became.

Ellie wished they could stop playing. Seeing famous people was exciting but Clara's know-all attitude was spoiling the fun. Then she finally noticed someone who looked familiar. "I'm sure I've seen that tall man somewhere before," she said.

"Of course you have," replied Clara, in her irritatingly superior voice. "That's James Dark. He plays Albert Blonde, secret agent."

"And I think *he* plays the villain," added Kate,

pointing excitedly at a small man on the opposite side of the crowd.

Clara looked even more superior. "Don't be silly. He's the lead guitarist from The Willows. Their latest song was number one in Sanbarosa for three whole weeks."

"I've got their CD at home," yelled Kate. "And I did recognize him, although I thought he was someone else. Does that mean I get a point?"

Before Clara had a chance to reply, a tall, elegant woman walked into the party, holding an equally elegant dog on a lead. "I definitely know him," cried Ellie. "It's Wilson the Wonder Dog."

"And Tina Truelove," added Clara, determined not to be outdone. "I adore their films."

"So do I," said Kate. "My favourite's the one where their plane crashes in the mountains and Wilson leads everyone to safety."

"Mine's the one where he saves the little girl from drowning," said Ellie.

"His latest film is best," declared Clara. "He stops a plot to take over the world and he rescues a baby from a burning building."

Kate looked puzzled. "I haven't seen that one."

Clara smiled smugly. "Of course you haven't," she explained. "It's not been released to ordinary people yet. But *I've* seen an advance copy."

Ellie gritted her teeth and growled silently to herself. She wished Clara would stop showing off. She really was the most irritating person Ellie had ever met.

Kate stared longingly at Wilson. "He looks so sweet and cuddly. I'd love to stroke him."

Princess Ellie's Summer Holiday

"Perhaps we can," said Ellie. She jumped to her feet and grabbed the last sausage from her plate. "Let's go and say 'hello'."

"I was just about to suggest that myself," said Clara. She pushed past Ellie and Kate and led the way over to Tina.

When they were only a few steps away, Wilson bounded towards the girls, nearly pulling Tina off her feet. Clara tried to stroke him as he rushed past, but he ignored her completely. The only person he was interested in was Ellie.

Tina looked at Ellie with a puzzled expression. "Hello there. I wonder why Wilson thinks you're so special?"

Chapter 5

Ellie smiled shyly. "I think he can smell this," she said, holding out the sausage. Wilson immediately jumped up and whisked it out of her hand. He bit it in two and gulped it down. Then he licked Ellie's hand all over to make sure there was nothing left behind.

"He certainly enjoyed that," laughed Tina. "But don't give him too many.

He mustn't get too fat for his films."

Ellie reached down and tickled Wilson's ears. Kate came up beside her and stroked his back. Clara could easily have walked round the other side of Ellie to reach the dog. But she didn't. She rudely pushed her way between the two girls and started to pat his head.

Wilson loved all the attention. He licked their faces and wagged his tail so hard that it became a blur. Then he rolled on his back to have his tummy tickled.

"He certainly likes all of you," said Tina. "Do you want to take him for a walk along the beach?"

"Yes, please," said all three girls together.

Tina handed the lead to Ellie, who was standing next to her.

Ellie was delighted. She ignored Clara's sulky stare and concentrated on Wilson. He bounced up and down, excited at the prospect of a walk.

"Have a lovely time," said Tina, as they set off. "But don't let him off his lead. He's not used to the island and I don't want him getting lost."

Princess Ellie's Summer Holiday

Ellie felt very proud as she strode across the sand with Wilson bounding along beside her. It felt wonderful to be in charge of such a beautiful dog. He was one of the most famous animals in the whole world and Tina had trusted *her* to look after him.

She planned to show Wilson the waves. But before they were halfway there, Clara snatched the lead out of her hand. "My turn now," declared the annoying princess. She ran off towards the sea with Ellie and Kate in pursuit.

"Wait for us," yelled Kate.

But Clara didn't wait. Instead she ran even faster. Wilson didn't behave as well for her as he had for Ellie. He tried to race ahead, pulling hard on the lead.

The Pony-Mad Princess

They caught up with Clara at the edge
of the water. Just as they arrived, she bent
down and started to fumble with Wilson's
neck.

At first, Ellie thought she was just stroking
him. Then she realized with horror what
Clara was really doing. She was unclipping
the lead.

"Don't do that!" yelled Ellie, grabbing desperately for Clara's hand. "You'll get us all into trouble."

"Let me go," cried Clara. She wriggled her hand, trying to free it from Ellie's grasp.

Ellie tightened her grip. "Only if you promise not to let him off his lead," she said.

Clara scowled. "But he's never on a lead in his films and he doesn't get lost in those."

At that moment, Wilson yelped and jumped backwards. His tail wasn't wagging now. It was tucked firmly between his legs.

Ellie looked round to see what had frightened him. It was a very small crab scuttling across the sand. It couldn't possibly hurt Wilson, but that hadn't stopped him being scared.

"I think Wilson's only acting in his films," said Ellie, as they stroked the dog to calm him down. "He's not as brave in real life and he's probably not as clever either."

"I don't care," said Kate. "He's still really sweet." As if to prove her right, the dog nuzzled her hand and wagged his tail. He was happy again now the crab had gone.

Clara wasn't. "You might as well have him now," she said, as she pushed the lead into Kate's hand. "Your friend's spoiled all the fun." She turned her back on them and stalked off towards her villa.

Ellie was pleased to see her go. The rest of the evening would be much more enjoyable without her. She just hoped Clara wouldn't behave so badly when they were riding.

Chapter 6

Breakfast the next morning was very different from at home. At the poolside restaurant, Ellie and Kate sat in the shade of a palm tree and ate fresh pineapple, mango and banana, washed down with coconut milk.

It was so delicious that they were tempted to have a second helping. But there wasn't time. They were determined not to be late for their first ride.

In fact, they were early and so was Clara. As they arrived, all three ponies looked over their stable doors to see what was happening. The grey pony whickered a welcome. So did the skewbald. But the pony with no mane just shook his head and went back inside.

"I really hope I don't have him," Ellie whispered to Kate. Now she had seen the grey pony again, she wanted him more than ever.

A short man with a suntanned face came out of the tack room and smiled warmly at the three girls. "Hello," he said. "I'm Simon, the horsemaster. And you must be Aurelia, Kate and Clara."

Clara pulled herself up to her full height

and looked indignant. "*Princess* Clara to you," she snapped.

Simon laughed. "Not here," he said. "We don't have formalities like that on this island."

Ellie took an immediate liking to him. "I like to be called Ellie," she said.

"That's fine with me," said Simon. He looked questioningly at Kate.

"Do you prefer to be called something else too? Bert, maybe, or Esmerelda?"

Kate giggled at the silly suggestion. "My name's fine just as it is."

Princess Ellie's Summer Holiday

Simon put down the bucket he was carrying and looked at the girls carefully. "Now the introductions are over, I'd better decide which pony each of you will have for the rest of your holiday."

"I want that one," announced Clara, pointing at the grey pony.

Simon shook his head. "It's not a question of who wants what," he explained. "I've got to make sure I match the right rider with the right pony. And that depends on how well you all ride."

Clara put on her superior expression again. "I'm an expert rider," she announced. "I have three ponies of my own at home, and one of them is the best showjumper in Sanbarosa."

Ellie sighed and silently wished Clara

would stop showing off. Then she turned to Simon and said, "I can ride quite well, but I've not been in any competitions."

"That doesn't matter," said Simon. "Can you walk, trot and canter?"

"Oh yes," said Ellie. "And I can jump a bit too."

"So can I," added Kate.

Simon turned to Clara and smiled. "Okay! As you're the best rider, you can have Mango."

"Is he the grey?" she asked.

"Oh no," laughed Simon, as he fetched the muddy brown pony. "This is Mango."

Clara stamped her foot angrily. "I don't want him. He's got no mane."

"That's not his fault," explained Simon, pushing the pony's lead rope into Clara's unwilling hand. "He's very bothered by the flies because his skin is so sensitive. I clip off his mane to stop them getting into it and making him itch."

He ignored Clara's crossness and turned to Kate. "You look as if you'd get on well with Patch. He's the skewbald pony in the stable at this end."

Kate squealed with delight as she went to fetch him. She'd got the pony that she wanted.

Ellie felt excited too. Surely there was only one pony left now – the beautiful grey with whom she'd fallen in love yesterday. She crossed her fingers behind her back, hoping there wasn't another pony hidden in one of the other stables.

Princess Ellie's Summer Holiday

To her relief, Simon buckled a headcollar on the grey pony and led him into the yard. "And that leaves you with Cloud," he laughed, as he handed her the rope.

Ellie took it with delight. Cloud was just as beautiful as she remembered. His mane was silky soft and his snow-white coat was as smooth as velvet.

But Clara was furious. "That's not fair!" she yelled. She marched across the yard with Mango and held out his rope to Simon. "I won't ride this horrible pony. I won't, I won't, I won't!"

Simon looked surprised at her show of temper. "Calm down," he said. "No one's going to make you ride if you don't want to. Just put Mango in his stable and go back to your parents."

"But I do want to ride," yelled Clara. "I just don't want to ride *him*." She glared at Mango. Then she pointed at Ellie and declared, "I want Cloud and if I don't get him, I'll cry." She screwed up her face and started to wail loudly.

Ellie could see she was pretending. The noise was quite realistic, but there were no tears.

Princess Ellie's Summer Holiday

Unfortunately, Simon was more easily fooled. He sighed and led Mango over to Ellie. "I hope you don't mind too much," he muttered, as he took Cloud away. "I didn't realize how much trouble this was going to cause."

Ellie watched miserably as he gave the grey pony to the other princess. It felt worse to have had Cloud and lost him than never to have had him in the first place. Was Clara going to spoil *everything* on this holiday?

Chapter 7

Ellie felt dismal as she tied Mango to the fence. He looked so strange without a mane. The place where it should have been was hard and bristly. Worse still, the pony didn't seem to like her. He constantly swished his tail and stamped his feet.

"Don't worry about him," said Simon, as he made sure she had tied the quick-release knot properly. "It's the flies he hates, not you."

He checked Kate and Clara's knots. Then he fetched boxes of grooming kit from the tack room and gave one to each of them. "I'll look after the ponies when you're not here," he explained. "But when you're at the stables, you'll have more fun if you care for them yourselves."

Once he'd made sure they knew what all the equipment was for, he left them to groom Mango, Cloud and Patch while he looked after his own horse – a chestnut mare called Calypso. "I'm happy to help if you want," he said. "Just call if you need me."

Ellie and Kate were used to grooming. They immediately started to brush their

65

ponies with long, well-practised strokes.
Clara looked less confident. She dabbed so
gently at Cloud's coat that the brush hardly
moved the hairs at all.

Ellie was still upset that Clara had taken
Cloud away. But she didn't want that to ruin
their holiday, so she tried to be friendly.
"You need to brush harder," she suggested.
"Stand closer to him and put your weight
behind the strokes. Look – like this." She
took the brush from Clara's hand and gave a
demonstration, sending up a cloud of dust
from Cloud's coat.

Clara scowled at her and snatched
back the brush. "You don't have to show
off," she complained. "I know perfectly well
how to brush a pony. I was just starting
gently."

Ellie felt hurt, but she didn't argue. She just went back and concentrated on Mango.

"Don't mind her," whispered Kate. "She's spoiled." But Ellie noticed Clara did follow her example. Perhaps she had listened after all.

Despite her initial problems, Clara was having a much easier time than Ellie. Cloud stood perfectly still while he was groomed. He even lowered his head to let her brush between his ears.

The Pony-Mad Princess

Mango's constant fidgeting made him much harder to groom. Ellie had to be careful not to get trodden on, or hit by his swishing tail. Having no mane to brush saved her some time. But cleaning out his feet took ages, because he kept putting them down almost as soon as she'd picked them up. As a result, Kate and Clara finished ages before she did.

Clara smiled her superior smile again. "I'm so glad I've got Cloud," she said. "He's the perfect pony."

Ellie tried to ignore her. It was bad enough that Clara had made her change ponies without the awful girl boasting about it.

When Mango was finally ready, Simon checked all the saddles and bridles were on properly. Then he made them line up side by side in the yard so he could help each of them mount.

Ellie's stomach churned with nerves as she watched Kate and Clara get on Patch and Cloud. Their ponies stood still for them, but she was sure Mango wouldn't. If he was so difficult to groom, he was going to be even harder to ride.

When her turn came, Simon walked over

and held Mango's bridle. "Cheer up," he said to Ellie. "You'll be fine. There's no need to look so worried."

His words made Ellie feel better. So did the fact that he was making Mango stand still. She picked up his reins, put her foot in the stirrup and swung herself onto his back. The brown pony flicked his ears back as he felt her weight on his saddle. But, to her relief, he didn't misbehave.

Simon and Calypso led the way out of the yard with Clara, while Ellie and Kate followed behind. They rode down a path with thick jungle on either side.

There were far more flies here than there had been at the stables and Mango hated them. He started to toss his large head up and down to keep them away. It worked

well, but it worried Ellie. It was the first time
she had ever ridden a pony that did that,
and she didn't know what to do.

She tried shortening the reins. Perhaps
that would stop him. But it didn't. It made
him worse. He tossed his head more than
ever, fighting the tight pull on his mouth as
well as the flies.

Ellie tried doing the opposite. She let the reins slip through her fingers so they hung long and loose. That didn't work either. As soon as Mango felt the pressure go from his mouth, he knew he was free to do whatever he wanted. And what he wanted to do was eat. He tossed his head once more. Then he swiftly dropped it to the ground and snatched a mouthful of grass.

The sudden movement took Ellie by surprise. She tried to grab his mane to steady herself. But there wasn't any mane. Her fingers closed on empty air.

72

Chapter 8

Luckily, she didn't fall. But her heart was beating at top speed, and her stomach was knotted with nerves again. She glanced ahead at Clara. At least the other princess wasn't laughing at her. She was too busy enjoying Cloud to realize Ellie was having trouble.

Kate was more observant. "Are you all

right?" she asked. She waited until Ellie
nodded. Then she added, "I wish Mango
was as lovely to ride as Patch."

"Mango's nicer than you think," said
Simon, who had ridden over to see what
was wrong. "He just takes a bit of getting
used to. Ride up at the front with me and I'll
see if I can help."

Ellie felt more confident beside Simon.
"I don't like it when he tosses his head,"
she admitted. "I've tried shortening the
reins and lengthening them, but nothing
seems to work."

Simon smiled. "Hold them just tight
enough so you can feel a gentle pressure on
his mouth," he explained. "Then move your
hands when he tosses his head so you keep
that pressure the same all the time. That

way you'll always be in control, but you won't jab him in the mouth."

Ellie listened carefully and tried to do as he said. It was tricky at first, but she soon got used to it. It was much more comfortable for her, and Mango seemed happier too. He still tossed his head a lot, but he felt more relaxed.

"That's better," laughed Simon. He looked behind him to check that Kate and Clara were all right. "Let's try going faster," he called and pushed Calypso into a trot.

Ellie tried to do the same. At first, Mango took no notice and kept walking. Then she pushed harder with her legs, and he finally broke into a bouncy trot, tossing his head in time with his front feet. He wasn't the most comfortable pony she had ever ridden, but at least he was behaving himself for now.

The path came out on the top of a hill. A large area of short, green grass stretched temptingly ahead of them. Simon urged Calypso into a canter and Ellie did the same.

She was delighted to find that Mango's canter was much more comfortable than his trot. She smiled happily as she relaxed in the saddle. Deep down inside, she still wished she was riding Cloud. But she was finally starting to enjoy herself. She loved the feel of the wind in her face and the sound of hooves drumming on the ground.

They stopped at the end of the grass and walked slowly to give the ponies a rest. Now Ellie was used to Mango tossing his head, she could pay more attention to her

surroundings. The island was very beautiful and completely different from the palace grounds.
Brightly coloured birds squawked at her from the bushes and she even spotted a monkey high up in the branches of a tree.

Eventually, Simon led them onto a patch of sand where someone had built a line of low, wooden jumps. "I thought it would be fun to finish the ride with these," he said.

"Great!" said Kate. "I love jumping."

"So do I," said Ellie. She paused and added in an anxious voice. "But does Mango?"

"Of course he does," replied Simon. "So does Patch. And Cloud is really good at it."

"Oh," said Clara without any enthusiasm. Her face was much whiter than it had been before.

Kate went first and jumped all the fences easily. "Patch is a wonderful jumper," she cried, as she trotted back to the others. "I hope Angel turns out to be as good as him."

It was Ellie's turn next. She felt a twinge of nerves again, as she cantered Mango towards the first fence. For a moment, she thought he would refuse. But she urged him on and he jumped over it easily.

Then he pricked his ears
forward and cleared the others
without any problems.

"Well done," said Simon. "Now it's
Cloud's turn."

Clara gulped, turned even whiter and
cantered the grey pony towards the first
fence. Cloud behaved perfectly as he flew
over each jump in turn. His rider had more
trouble. She lost her right stirrup at the first
jump, her left stirrup at the second one and
the reins at the third. By the time she

reached the end, she was clinging onto
Cloud's neck to stop herself falling off.

Simon raced after her. "Are you all right?"
he called.

Clara said nothing until Cloud stopped.
Then she swiftly put her feet back in her
stirrups, sorted out her reins and sat up
straight again. "I'm fine," she insisted, as she
trotted over to join the others.

"I don't understand," said Ellie. "You said you'd won lots of showjumping competitions."

"No, I didn't," snapped Clara. "I said my pony had won them."

"Isn't that the same thing?" asked Kate.

For the first time since they'd met, Clara looked embarrassed. "No," she admitted quietly. "Someone else was riding him."

Ellie was tempted to laugh, but she didn't. She was glad that Kate didn't either. Surely, Clara must realize she'd made a fool of herself. There was no need to make her feel even worse.

Chapter 9

Clara avoided them on the way back. She rode on ahead with Simon, leaving the other two girls to ride together. Ellie liked that arrangement. It felt like riding at home, except it was much hotter and they were surrounded by jungle.

When they reached the stables, they took off the ponies' saddles and bridles, brushed their backs and turned them loose in the field. Mango, Patch and Cloud immediately ambled over to the shade of the shelter.

Simon smiled at Kate and Ellie as they hung their saddles in the tack room. "You two ride very well."

"What about me?" asked Clara. "I'm a better rider than either of them."

Ellie stared at her in disbelief. Hadn't she learned anything from her dreadful display of jumping?

"I'm afraid you're not," said Simon. "But don't worry. All three of you ride well enough to take your ponies out without me. There's just one rule. None of you must go riding alone."

"Why not?" asked Kate.

"Because if you're out by yourself, there's no one to fetch help if something goes wrong," explained Simon.

"That's not fair," moaned Clara. "They've got each other to ride with, but I'm on my own."

"Don't worry," said Simon. "I can go with

you if you don't want to go with Ellie and Kate."

His words seemed to cheer Clara up a little. "I want to ride tomorrow morning," she ordered.

"Sorry," said Simon. "That's one time I can't manage. Don's asked me to go to some horse sales on the mainland. I won't be back until after dark."

Clara glared at him angrily. As she opened her mouth to argue, Ellie nudged Kate with her elbow. "Let's go," she whispered. "I don't want to see another tantrum."

"Neither do I," said Kate. Then they ran out of the yard together, leaving Clara arguing with Simon.

*

The Pony-Mad Princess

When they got back
to the villa, they found
Higginbottom was
getting into the
holiday mood.
He was wearing his
black evening suit,
as usual. But he had
taken off his shoes
and socks, rolled up
his trousers and put a
straw sun hat on his head.

"The King and Queen have already had
lunch and left for the beach," he said.
"They hope you'll join them later."

Ellie and Kate changed into T-shirts
and shorts and sat down in the shade of
the garden. Higginbottom brought them

prawn sandwiches and crystal glasses of fresh
lemonade. While they ate
and drank, they made plans.

It was very

hot now

and the

ponies

had already done
enough work for today.
So they decided to spend
the rest of the afternoon by
the sea. Then they would go riding again
tomorrow after breakfast.

"That's when Clara wanted to go," said
Kate.

Ellie groaned. "I hope she doesn't ask
to go with us. It will be much more fun
without her."

The Pony-Mad Princess

As soon as they had finished lunch, they crammed their swimming things into their beach bags and set off to join the King and Queen. But they couldn't resist stopping on the way at the do-it-yourself ice-cream bar.

They each took an empty ice-cream cone. Then they walked along the counter, helping themselves to everything they wanted. Ellie chose strawberry ice cream smothered with maple syrup and chopped nuts.

Princess Ellie's Summer Holiday

Kate preferred toffee ice cream topped with chocolate sprinkles. She was just adding a few tiny pieces of fudge when Clara ran up to them.

"Are you riding tomorrow?" she asked, as she grabbed a cone.

"We're going in the morning," said Kate.

"You can come with us if you want," added Ellie, hesitantly. She knew it would be mean not to offer. But she hoped Clara would say no.

"I don't need to," said Clara, as she piled three huge scoops of chocolate ice cream into her cone. "I've just arranged to do something much more exciting after breakfast."

"What is it?" asked Ellie and Kate together.

Clara paused while she drowned her ice cream in strawberry sauce. Then she stuck her nose in the air and smiled her superior smile. "I'm not telling you," she said. "It's a secret."

Chapter 10

Ellie was intrigued. So was Kate. They hung around for a while, hoping Clara would change her mind and tell them the secret. But she didn't. Instead, she glanced scornfully at their bags. "Are you going swimming?" she asked.

"We're going snorkelling to look at the fish," said Kate, pulling out her snorkel and mask.

"How terribly boring," said Clara. She squirted cream onto her cone so fast that it hit the top and splattered in all directions. "I'm going waterskiing," she announced, completely ignoring the mess. "You can watch me if you like. I'm one of the best waterskiers in Sanbarosa."

"I wonder if she really is," said Kate, as Clara marched off along the beach.

"I don't know," said Ellie, wiping a blob of cream from her nose. "I'm much more interested in what she's planning to do tomorrow. What can possibly be more exciting than riding?" They wandered across the sand, eating their ice creams while they looked for the King and Queen. They found them relaxing in the shade of a huge, striped umbrella. They had both swapped their usual, heavy royal robes for lightweight cotton ones, and the Queen had perched a pair of sunglasses on her nose.

"I'm glad you're here," said the King. "I need some help with my sand palace." He pointed to an unimpressive heap of sand further down the beach.

"Does it have to be a palace?" asked Ellie. "A sand pony would be much more fun."

"But it would have to be lying down," pointed out Kate. "Sand legs are much too difficult."

"All right," said the King. "A sand pony it is." He leaped to his feet, picked up a silver bucket and spade and ran across the beach.

Ellie and Kate followed him and set to work. Soon, they were all laughing and joking as they heaped up the damp sand and patted it into shape. They found a large pebble for the pony's eye, and they decorated its mane and tail with lines of tiny shells.

When they had finished, they stepped back and looked proudly at their work.

Princess Ellie's Summer Holiday

The Queen came down to admire it too.
"It's magnificent," she said. "Now I think it's
time we all cooled off in the sea."

"Splendid idea," said the King. He took
off his robe, straightened his ermine-
trimmed swimming trunks and plunged into
the water.

The Pony-Mad Princess

The Queen was more cautious. She walked down to the edge of the sea and stepped gingerly into the shallow waves. A maid held up the bottom of her robe to stop it getting wet while she paddled.

Ellie and Kate fetched their snorkels, masks and flippers and followed the King into the water. Soon, they were swimming

Princess Ellie's Summer Holiday

face down across the surface of the sea, looking at the beautiful underwater world beneath them.

Clara was wrong. Snorkelling wasn't boring at all. Ellie had never seen so many different kinds of fish. The smallest flitted about in groups, their scales flashing silver in the sunlight. Between them swam bright blue fish with long fins like scarves and red fish with white stripes. Starfish glided silently across the sandy bottom and a baby turtle swam past, using its tiny flippers to push itself through the water.

Suddenly, the King tapped Ellie and Kate on

the shoulder. "That looks as if it might be fun," he said, as they lifted their faces out of the water.

They stood up and looked where he was pointing. A speedboat was roaring past, towing a small figure on waterskis.

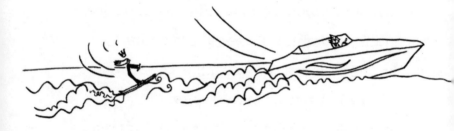

"It's Clara," cried Ellie, waving at the other princess. "She really can do it."

Clara let go of the rope with one hand and waved back. But the movement made her lose her balance. She slipped sideways, fell over and landed with a splash in the sea.

"She's not quite as good as she said,"

giggled Kate, as they watched her being pulled into the boat.

That was the last they saw of Clara that day. They didn't see her at breakfast the next morning either. And they were so busy looking forward to their ride they'd forgotten about her secret. As soon as they had finished eating, they set off for the stables. They were almost at the clump of palm trees that hid the turning, when they spotted a familiar figure coming the other way.

"Oh, no," groaned Kate. "It's Clara. I wonder what she's going to show off about this morning."

Ellie couldn't face that superior smile again, and she didn't want to be ordered about any more. "Quick, let's hide," she

cried, as she jumped between two large
bushes and pulled Kate in after her.

They crouched behind the leaves,
hoping they wouldn't be discovered.
As the other princess came closer and
closer, Ellie realized she was crying.
And this time there were real tears.

"I wonder what's happened," whispered
Kate.

Princess Ellie's Summer Holiday

"It must be something awful," Ellie whispered back. Clara didn't look superior or bossy any more. She just looked utterly miserable. Ellie bit her lip anxiously as she watched her. "It's no good," she said. "We've got to do something. I can't bear to see her so upset."

Kate nodded. "Neither can I. Come on!"

They stepped out in front of Clara, trying to look as if there was a good reason why they had been in the bushes. "What's happened?" asked Ellie.

Clara stared at them with eyes red from crying. "It's Wilson," she sobbed. "Tina let me take him out for a walk."

"So that was your secret!" declared Kate.

Clara sniffed loudly and nodded. "I let him off his lead. Tina told me not to, but I thought he'd have more fun if I did. And I was sure he would come back when I called him."

"Did he?" asked Ellie, although she could guess the answer.

"No!" wailed Clara, waving the empty lead in front of their faces. "He ran away so fast that I couldn't keep up with him. Now he's lost and I'm in big trouble."

Ellie knew what being in big trouble felt like, so she really wanted to help. But Wilson could be anywhere on the whole island. How on earth could they find him?

Chapter 11

Clara sniffed again and wiped her nose with the back of her hand. "It's no good," she sobbed. "I'll have to tell Tina I've lost Wilson."

"Don't do that yet," said Kate. "Perhaps we can find him if we all look together."

Clara shook her head. "He ran away too fast. We'll never catch up with him."

Princess Ellie's Summer Holiday

"We might if we take the ponies," said Ellie. "They can go much faster than him."

To her surprise, for once the other princess didn't reject her idea. Instead, she gave a half-hearted smile and nodded in agreement. "I suppose we'd have a chance," she admitted.

"That's settled then," said Kate. "We'll get the ponies ready, while you get your riding hat."

Clara raced off towards her villa. She looked more cheerful now Ellie and Kate had offered to help. They watched her disappear down the path. Then they turned and ran the other way, heading towards the stables.

They found all three ponies dozing in the thatched shelter. Patch and Cloud came when they called them. Mango was more reluctant to leave the shade. Ellie had to go inside to fetch him.

There wasn't time to groom them properly, so Ellie and Kate quickly brushed their backs. Then they fetched the saddles and bridles from the tack room and put them on.

Ellie had just finished fastening Cloud's bridle when Clara ran into the yard, dressed in her riding clothes. "Thanks," she muttered, as she seized hold of the grey pony's reins. "I'll take him now."

Handing over the grey pony reminded Ellie of losing him the day before. But she tried to ignore the twinge of jealousy. At least Clara had said "thanks". That was a huge improvement on her previous behaviour, and they needed to work together to find Wilson.

As soon as they were all settled on their ponies, the girls trotted out of the yard. Clara went in front, leading them along the route

she'd taken with Wilson. Eventually, she
stopped in a small clearing surrounded
by dense jungle and pointed along a
path between the trees.

"This is where I last saw him. He ran along there, but I was too out of breath to follow him any further."

"We'd better hurry," said Kate. "He must be well ahead of us by now."

They pushed the ponies into a canter. Their hooves flew across the ground much faster than Wilson could run. Mango tossed his head as usual, but Ellie was used to that now. She was even starting to enjoy his bumpy stride, although she still looked enviously at Cloud from time to time.

As they reached the top of a low hill, Clara pulled the grey pony to a halt. "There he is," she cried.

Ellie and Kate rode their ponies up beside her and looked in the direction she was pointing. A long way ahead, Wilson was busy sniffing a bush. His tail was wagging at full speed.

"Here, Wilson!" yelled Clara at the top of her voice. "Come here, boy!"

Wilson stopped sniffing. He looked up and took a step towards them. For a moment, Ellie thought he was going to come to them.

Then a small, brown animal shot out of the bushes just in front of him.
It wasn't a rabbit – its ears were much too short. It looked more like a large guinea pig.

Whatever it was, it didn't like dogs. It took one look at Wilson and ran back into the jungle. The Wonder Dog barked excitedly. Then he hurtled after it and swiftly vanished amongst the undergrowth.

"Quick! After him!" cried Ellie. She pushed Mango into a gallop and raced off in pursuit. If they didn't hurry, they would lose Wilson again.

Chapter 12

Ellie, Kate and Clara bent low over their ponies' necks as they galloped down the path. But they had to stop when they reached the place where they had last seen Wilson. They knew he had run into the jungle. But they didn't know which way he'd gone.

"Can you see any tracks?" said Kate.

Ellie looked around and shook her head. There were no paw prints, no crushed plants and no dog hairs caught on twigs – nothing at all to show where Wilson had been.

"We've lost him!" wailed Clara. There was a hint of panic in her voice.

Then they heard an excited bark. "He's over there," shouted Ellie. "It sounds as if he's still chasing that little animal." She turned Mango in the direction of the sound and led the way into the jungle. Clara and Kate followed close behind.

They could only ride slowly now. There was no path, so they had to force their way between the plants and trees. Ellie held her reins in one hand and used the other one to push away the branches.

Princess Ellie's Summer Holiday

Each time they heard another bark, they checked they were going in the right direction. But Ellie was worried. Although the ponies could run faster than the dog on open ground, he could wriggle through the jungle more easily than they could. Would they ever manage to catch him?

Suddenly Wilson gave a high-pitched yelp. The sound sent a tingle of fear down Ellie's spine. He didn't sound excited any more. He sounded scared.

"I hope he's not hurt," said Kate.

"If he is, it's all my fault," wailed Clara.

Wilson yelped again and again. Ellie was sure he was calling for help. She tried to go faster, but the jungle made that impossible. Mango was already doing the best he could.

Then they pushed their way between two tall trees and stepped out onto another path. It ran along the edge of a steep, narrow valley with a fast-flowing river at the bottom. A wooden bridge led from one side to the other, high above the water.

"Which way now?" asked Kate.

As if in answer, Wilson gave a couple

more yelps, followed by a long, plaintive howl. It was the most miserable sound Ellie had ever heard, and it was coming from somewhere across the river.

"He must have gone over the bridge," said Clara.

"We'd better do the same," replied Ellie. She made Mango walk towards it. But when he reached the edge of the wooden planks, he stopped dead.

"Walk on," said Ellie firmly. She squeezed her legs as hard as she could against his sides.

Mango didn't budge. He braced his front legs, refusing to step forward.

"What's wrong with him?" called Kate from the back of the line.

"I don't know," said Ellie. She kicked Mango with her heels. This time the pony moved. But he didn't go forwards. He stepped backwards and snorted with fear.

"That pony's a pain," grumbled Clara. She started to push past on Cloud. "I bet he's just worried about flies again. You'd better let us go in front."

"No!" cried Ellie. She reached out and grabbed the grey pony's bridle to stop him.

"Let me go!" yelled Clara. "You're not the only person capable of leading."

"I know," said Ellie. "But I don't think Mango is being silly. I think he's frightened of something, and we ought to find out what it is." She jumped down from the brown pony's back, keeping hold of his reins. Then she slowly stepped forward onto the bridge.

She put her foot down carefully. The wood groaned slightly, but it seemed firm enough.

Princess Ellie's Summer Holiday

She took another step. That was all right too. But on the third step, the wood splintered under her weight, and her foot plunged downwards into empty space.

Ellie screamed as she fell towards the hole. She grabbed for the rail of the bridge. But it was too far away.

Chapter 13

Ellie's eyes widened in fear as she looked down at the rushing water far below her. She tightened her grip on Mango's reins. They were the only thing that might save her now. That's when she felt the pony pull back on them, helping her to safety. He seemed to realize she was in danger.

She struggled back to the bank and sat

down, still shaking with fright.

Kate jumped down from Patch and ran over to her. "Are you all right?" she asked.

"Yes," said Ellie. "Thanks to Mango." She patted the pony's muddy brown neck and stroked his face.

"Perhaps we should go back and get help," said Clara.

Wilson howled again. "That will take ages," said Ellie. "We could help him much quicker ourselves if only we could get across the river."

Kate shuddered. "Not on that bridge," she said. "It's too dangerous."

"There's no other way to get across," said Clara.

"There might be somewhere further upstream," suggested Ellie. "Let's ride upriver a little way to see. And if we don't find anywhere soon, we'll go for help."

They rode off together along the path. Wilson's dismal howls added urgency to their search. The further they went, the less deep the valley became. The sight made Ellie feel more hopeful. "Just a bit further," she said. "Perhaps there'll be a good crossing place soon."

But there wasn't. As they rode round the next bend, they saw a high rocky cliff straight ahead of them. A huge waterfall tumbled down it into a deep, dark pool that fed the raging river.

"It's beautiful," said Kate, as she stared at the falling water. The sunlight shining through the spray sent a rainbow arching across the cliff.

"It's a nuisance," said Ellie. "We can't go any further upstream. The cliff is in the way."

"And the river is still too difficult to cross," said Clara. "We've no choice now. We'll have to go back."

"Maybe not," said Ellie, thoughtfully. She could vaguely remember something she'd seen about waterfalls on TV. If the same was true of this one, it might solve their problem.

She rode Mango as close as she could to the cliff. Then she crossed her fingers and peered along the rocky wall. To her delight, she saw exactly what she'd hoped for. Behind the curtain of falling water was a large space. It had been hollowed out by thousands of years of spray.

Ellie beckoned the others over. "It's like a tunnel," she said. "We can walk through it to the other side."

"Are you sure it's safe?" asked Clara.

"I think so," said Ellie. "The floor's flat and there's plenty of room."

They jumped off the ponies and led them towards the tunnel. Ellie went first with Mango. The brown pony hesitated at the entrance.

Princess Ellie's Summer Holiday

Then he flicked his ears forward and
followed Ellie onto the wide, rocky ledge.
Kate and Clara followed close behind with
Patch and Cloud.

It was easy to see where they were going.
The sun shone through the falling water,
making patterns on the rocky wall. It was
much harder to talk. Inside the tunnel,

the roar of the waterfall was deafening.
It drowned out everything they said.

There was so much spray that it was like
walking through a rainstorm. By the time
they reached the other side, they were all
soaked to the skin.

But they knew they had to hurry. Wilson
needed them. So they mounted quickly and
galloped back along the river. Soon their
wet clothes were steaming in the hot sun.
And by the time they reached the bridge,
they were almost dry.

Wilson was still howling. The sound
seemed to be coming from a steep slope
covered with grass and bushes. But there
was no sign of the dog.

Kate looked puzzled. "Where is he?"
she asked.

Princess Ellie's Summer Holiday

"He must be around here somewhere," said Clara.

Ellie felt just as confused. She scratched the back of her neck thoughtfully and stared at the slope. Then she noticed a pile of rocks at the bottom and ran forward to investigate. As she got closer, she saw they were blocking a hole. It looked like the entrance to a burrow.

The howling had stopped now. Wilson was whining pitifully instead and the noise was coming from inside the hole. Ellie could just see the tip of his nose through a gap at the top of the rocks.

The gap was far too small for him to wriggle through. And the rocks were too heavy for him to move. There was no way Wilson could get out of the hole by himself. He was completely stuck.

Chapter 14

"I don't understand," said Kate. "If he can't get out, how did he get in there in the first place?"

"He must have chased that strange animal into it," suggested Clara.

Kate still looked puzzled. "But he can't have done. That gap's not big enough."

Ellie bent down and examined the area

around the hole. "I don't think it was this small when he got here." She pointed at fresh marks on the slope. "The rocks used to be up there. Wilson must have knocked them when he ran past. They tumbled down and blocked the entrance after he went in."

"Be careful," said Kate. "If any other rocks fall down, you might get hurt."

Ellie looked up carefully. "There aren't any," she said. "It's quite safe. All we've got to worry about is getting Wilson out."

They set to work with enthusiasm, moving the rocks away as quickly as they could. Clearing the entrance was harder than they expected. The rocks were rough and heavy. Soon their fingers were sore and their arms ached.

They wanted to rest, but they knew that

they couldn't. They had to get the dog out soon. He was becoming more and more upset. If he panicked, he might hurt himself or bring the roof of the burrow tumbling down on top of him.

"Wilson never needs rescuing in his films," said Clara, as she struggled to move one of the larger boulders. "He's always rescuing other people."

"But this is real life," said Ellie. She grabbed hold of the other side of the boulder and together they managed to heave it out of the way.

"Poor old Wilson," said Kate. "He's not really a Wonder Dog at all."

There was only one rock left now. But it was much larger than the others. It blocked most of the hole all by itself. Wilson could get his nose past it, but there wasn't room for the rest of him. The girls had no choice. They had to move the rock in order to set him free.

Clara gave it an experimental tug. "It's really heavy. I can't shift it at all."

"Perhaps we can if we all lift together," suggested Kate. But that didn't work either. This rock was smoother than the others. It was hard to lift it up when they couldn't get a good grip on it.

Ellie bit her lip thoughtfully. Then she had an idea. "We don't have to lift it at all. We only have to slide it far enough forward to let Wilson wriggle past." She grabbed a branch from the undergrowth and pushed it under one end of the rock. Then she tried to lever it away from

the entrance. The branch snapped. So did the next one she tried and the next. "You might as well give up," sighed Clara. "That's not going to work."

"But digging might," said Kate. "If we dig

a hollow under the front of the rock, we might be able to roll it forward."

The three girls kneeled down and scrabbled at the earth with their sore fingers. But the ground was hard and stony. It was impossible to dig a hole in it with their bare hands.

"We need a spade," said Ellie.

"Or a pickaxe," added Clara.

"Or a rope," said Kate. "If we had a rope, we might be able to pull the rock forwards."

Ellie slumped down on the grass to ease her aching back. Everything looked hopeless. They couldn't rescue Wilson without the right equipment. But she hated the idea of giving up when they were so close to success.

She stared up at the trees and had an idea. "Look at those creepers up there," she said excitedly, as she leaped to her feet. "We could use one of those as a rope."

"Brilliant!" said Kate.

"Are you sure they're strong enough?" asked Clara.

"No," said Ellie. "But it's worth a try." They chose the longest creeper they could see and pulled it down from the trees. Then Ellie made a big loop in one end, passed it over the top of the rock and pulled it tight round the middle.

Wilson started barking loudly again. "Don't worry, Wilson," said Kate. "You'll soon be free."

Ellie, Kate and Clara took hold of the

rope and started to pull. They heaved and tugged until their arms ached. But the rock still didn't move.

Chapter 15

Clara began to cry again. "It's hopeless," she wailed. "We've tried everything, but nothing works. We can't let Wilson suffer any more. We've got to go for help."

Behind them, Mango stamped his feet and snorted at the flies. Ellie turned and looked at him. He had saved her from falling when the bridge broke. Perhaps there was a chance he could help again.

"Don't give up yet," she said. She took the dog lead from Clara and clipped it to one of the metal rings on the front of the brown pony's saddle. Then she slipped the creeper through the loop at the other end and tied it so it couldn't slip out. "Walk back, Mango," she said.

At first, Mango just looked puzzled. Then he seemed to realize what he had to do. He took one step backwards, then another. As he gradually walked away, the dog lead tightened and pulled on the creeper. Mango braced himself against the strain and kept going.

"Come on. Let's join in," called Ellie. She grabbed hold of the creeper and started to pull. So did Kate and Clara.

The extra help from Mango made all the difference. The rock finally started to move. Very, very slowly it slid forward away from the hole. As it did so, the gap between the rock and the edge of the hole grew bigger and bigger.

Wilson yelped with delight and wriggled through. He rushed up to the girls, wagging his tail and jumping up to lick their faces.

Clara quickly grabbed hold of his collar to make sure he didn't run away again.

"We've done it," she squealed. Then she smiled at Ellie and Kate. "I can't thank you enough. I'd never have found him without you."

"Don't worry about it," said Kate. "That's what friends are for."

"Anyway, it's Mango who deserves the

real thanks," added Ellie. She stroked the pony's face lovingly. "He was fantastic."

"Now let's get Wilson home," said Kate. "Tina will be wondering where he is."

"I'll walk with him," said Clara. "His lead is too short to hold while I'm riding."

"That's easily dealt with," laughed Ellie. She tied a creeper to the end of the lead and handed it to Clara. "Now let's get going."

"That's a good idea," said Kate. "We've got a long ride ahead."

"And a whole holiday to enjoy," added Ellie. "It's going to be much more fun now we're all good friends."

Clara started to put her foot in Cloud's stirrup, ready to mount. Then she stopped, took her foot out, and led the grey pony over to Ellie instead. "I'm sorry I was so mean to you yesterday," she said, pushing his reins into Ellie's hands. "And to prove it, I want you to have Cloud."

Ellie looked at the grey pony and ran her fingers through his snow-white mane. He was still as beautiful as she'd first thought, but that didn't seem so important any more. "No, thanks," she said, as she handed his reins back to Clara. "I'd rather have Mango."

She stroked the brown pony's nose lovingly. "He saved Wilson by moving that rock, he saved me from falling into the river and he saved all of us from that dangerous bridge."

Mango snorted and nuzzled her arm. Then he shook his head and swished his tail, as if keeping the flies away was more

important than remembering how clever
he was.

Ellie laughed. Then she threw her arms
round the brown pony's neck and hugged
him. "Wilson isn't a Wonder Dog," she said.
"But Mango really is a Wonder Pony."

Dear Reader,

Are you as pony-mad as Princess Ellie?
I am. I've loved ponies for as long as I can
remember. But I didn't get the pony I
dreamed of until I was grown up.

When I was a child, I had to make do
with reading about ponies and making up
imaginary stories about them. Maybe
that's why I write pony books now.

I hope you enjoy Princess Ellie's
adventures and, because I remember how
much I loved learning about ponies, there
are some fantastic facts and fun quiz
questions just for you in the following
pages...

Love, Diana
xx

Pony-Mad Fun & Facts

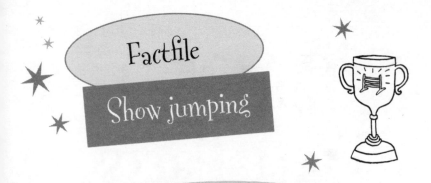

Factfile

Show jumping

Jumping competitions are a great test
of skills for both horse and rider. They are fun
to watch too! Here is an explanation
of some of the terms you might hear
associated with show jumping.

FAULTS: These are penalty points given for
knocking down a fence, refusing to jump and
other mistakes.

TIME FAULTS: Some competitions have a time
limit for the course. If you take longer than
that, you earn time faults.

KNOCK-DOWNS: You get the same number
of faults for knocking down one pole as you
do for demolishing the whole jump. In most
competitions, the penalty is four faults.

REFUSALS: A refusal is when your horse stops in front of the jump or runs out by swerving to avoid the jump. You are allowed to try again but you are eliminated if you get too many refusals. In big competitions, you're usually only allowed two refusals but smaller shows may let you try three times.

CLEAR ROUND: If you don't get any faults at all, you've jumped a clear round.

JUMP-OFF: If more than one horse gets a clear round, there's a jump-off to decide who has won. The jumps are higher for this, but there are usually fewer of them. If the jump-off is against the clock, the horses are timed so they have to jump quickly as well as accurately.

Princess Ellie's Pony-Mad Quiz

Do you know your **saddle** from your **stirrup**? Or which pony Ellie rides in **Onataki**? Test your knowledge of Princess Ellie's world with this quiz!

1. Princess Clara comes from:
a) Sanbarosa
b) Onataki
c) Andirovia

2. Patch is what type of pony?
a) A grey
b) A piebald
c) A skewbald

3. Why is Mango's mane clipped short?
a) To stop Mango getting too hot
b) To stop flies getting in it
c) To make Mango easier to groom

4. It's possible to tell a pony's age by looking at:
a) Its feet
b) Its ears
c) Its teeth

5. The back of a saddle is called:
a) The cantle
b) The canter
c) The cantaloupe

6. While snorkelling, Ellie and Kate see a baby:
a) Dolphin
b) Turtle
c) Shark

7. The beautiful grey pony Clara rides is called:
a) Cloud
b) Rain
c) Thunder

Turn the page to
find out the answers...

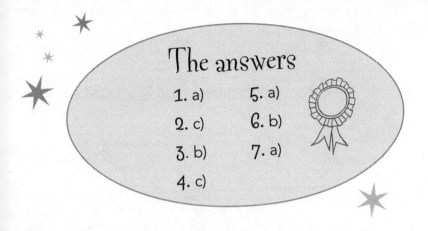

The answers

1. a)   5. a)

2. c)   6. b)

3. b)   7. a)

4. c)

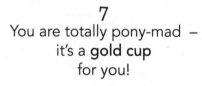

Tot up your total to see just how pony-mad you are...

1-3
A good try.

4-6
Great knowledge and a big rosette!

7
You are totally pony-mad –
it's a **gold cup**
for you!

Did you know...
Handy hints about
pony behaviour

As Ellie and Kate know, ponies don't always do exactly what you want them to! But they are not always being naughty. Sometimes there are good reasons for their behaviour.

* In the wild, ponies have to keep themselves safe from animals that might attack them. So it is natural for them to be cautious about sudden movements and to run away from anything they think might be dangerous.

* Ponies live in herds so they instinctively follow a leader they trust. Your pony is more likely to do what you want if he trusts you to be his leader.

* One way ponies decide who is leader is by seeing who can make another move their feet. When your pony pushes you with his head, he may be seeing if he can make you move.

* Ponies are very good at reading each other's body language and they can read yours too. They are more likely to do what you want if you are confident and calm than if you are hesitant and nervous.

* Ponies feel safer in a group because they are herd animals. As a result, they may become anxious if they are left in a field on their own.

* When ponies buck, they lift their backs and kick out with their hind legs. Sometimes they buck out of high spirits, but it can be a sign of a sore back or a badly fitting saddle.

* Flies are a big nuisance and some of them bite. Ponies toss their heads, swish their tails and kick at their stomachs to keep them away. Out in the field, two ponies may stand head to tail to help protect each other from flies.

Read on for a sneak preview of
Princess Ellie's next adventure...

Chapter 1

"Can I stop now?" asked Princess Ellie.

"Certainly not," replied Miss Stringle. "Your holiday does not begin until your lessons are over, and there is still half an hour to go."

"But John will be here soon," pleaded Ellie.

"No, he won't," said her teacher, firmly.

"Prince John is not due to arrive for another hour. Now please get on with your work. Princesses should not argue."

Ellie sighed. She was tired of her history lesson. She was tired of studying in the palace library, and she was tired of its rows of old books stored in ancient bookcases. She longed to be out in the sunshine with her ponies. Perhaps Miss Stringle would change her mind once she'd finished the worksheet.

The long list of questions was all about princesses from the past. She'd been working on them all afternoon. Thank goodness there were only three left.

She chewed the end of her pencil as she turned the gold-edged pages of *The Complete Guide to the Royal Family*. The huge book was packed with boring information. It said when people were born and when they died, but it never mentioned whether they liked ponies as much as Ellie did.

She quickly discovered that Princess Marissa's older brother was called James and that Princess Andromeda had married King Proctor the Proud of Protavia. It took her much longer to work out that Princess Traviata was her great-great-great-great-aunt.

She wrote down the last answer and waved her paper in the air. "I've finished," she declared. "Can I stop now?"

"Not quite yet," replied her teacher. She pointed at the books spread out in front of Ellie. "I want you to put those back in their right places while I mark your work. Then I can see if you've remembered what I taught you about how the library is organized."

Ellie groaned. She hadn't listened to Miss Stringle droning on and on about the library. She'd been far too busy daydreaming about her five beautiful ponies. Now she had no idea where the books belonged.

She stacked them on top of each other, picked them up and set off round the room. As she walked, she looked at the shelves carefully, searching for spaces that might give her a clue.

The first gap she spotted was high above her head. As she stood on tiptoe to push a book into it, the rest of the pile wobbled.

She tried to steady it, and she almost succeeded. But one book slid off. It tumbled to the ground, slid across the shiny wooden floor and vanished under a bookcase.

Luckily, Miss Stringle didn't notice. She

was still busy with her marking. So Ellie dumped the other books on a table. Then she lay down and looked under the nearest set of shelves.

The book was right at the back, resting against the wall. She reached out to grab it and felt something long and soft brush against her fingers.

Ellie pulled her hand away in surprise. Then she peered under the bookcase again and spotted a piece of red ribbon dangling from the back of the bottom shelf. "I wonder how long that's been there," she thought. The maids would never have noticed it while they were sweeping.

This was much more interesting than her lesson. She forgot about the book for a moment and pulled gently on the ribbon. It didn't move. She pulled again a bit harder. This time it shifted a little and then got stuck.

Ellie gave it a short, sharp tug and the ribbon finally pulled free. As it slid out of its hiding place, she saw for the first time that it was tied round a tightly rolled scroll of paper.

"Princess Aurelia!" shouted Miss Stringle. "Get up at once. Princesses do not grovel on the floor."

"I'm sorry," said Ellie, wishing her teacher wouldn't use her real name. "I was just fetching a book I dropped." She decided not to mention the scroll. That was her secret, and she wasn't ready to share it yet.

To find out what happens next read

✳ **Princess Ellie's** ✳
Treasure Hunt

Don't miss a single sparkly story!

The Pony-Mad Princess

Now also available as ebooks

Princess Ellie to the Rescue
ISBN: 9781409565963
Can Ellie save her beloved pony, Sundance, when he goes missing?

Princess Ellie's Secret
ISBN: 9781409565970
Ellie comes up with a secret plan to stop Shadow from being sold.

A Puzzle for Princess Ellie
ISBN: 9781409565987
Why won't Rainbow go down the spooky woodland path?

Princess Ellie's Starlight Adventure
ISBN: 9781409565994
Hoofprints appear on the palace lawn and Ellie has to find the culprit.

Princess Ellie's Moonlight Mystery
ISBN: 9781409566007
Ellie is enjoying pony camp, until she hears noises in the night.

A Surprise for Princess Ellie
ISBN: 9781409566014
Ellie sets off in search of adventure, but ends up with a big surprise.

Princess Ellie's Holiday Adventure
ISBN: 9781409566021
Ellie and Kate go to visit Prince John, and get lost in the snow!

Princess Ellie and the Palace Plot
ISBN: 9781409566038
Can Ellie's pony, Starlight, help her uncover the palace plot?

Princess Ellie's Christmas
ISBN: 9781409566045
Ellie's plan for the perfect Christmas present goes horribly wrong...

Princess Ellie Saves the Day
ISBN: 9781409566052
Can Ellie save the day when one of her ponies gets ill?

Princess Ellie's Summer Holiday
ISBN: 9781409566069
Wilfred the Wonder Dog is missing and it's up to Ellie to find him.

Princess Ellie's Treasure Hunt
ISBN: 9781409566076
Will Ellie find the secret treasure buried in the palace grounds?

Princess Ellie's Perfect Plan
ISBN: 9781409556787
Can Ellie find the perfect plan to stop her best friend from leaving?